GORT
THE DEADLY SNATCHER

With special thanks to Tabitha Jones

For Edward Pearce

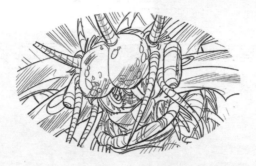

ORCHARD BOOKS

First published in Great Britain in 2016 by The Watts Publishing Group

3 5 7 9 10 8 6 4

Text © 2016 Beast Quest Limited.
Cover and inside illustrations by Artful Doodlers with special thanks to Bob and Justin
© Orchard Books 2016

Series created by Beast Quest Limited, London

A CIP catalogue record for this book is available from the British Library.

ISBN 978 1 40834 090 5

Printed in Great Britain

The paper and board used in this book are made from wood from responsible sources

Orchard Books
An imprint of Hachette Children's Group
Part of The Watts Publishing Group Limited
Carmelite House, 50 Victoria Embankment, London EC4Y 0DZ

An Hachette UK Company
www.hachette.co.uk
www.hachettechildrens.co.uk

GORT
THE DEADLY SNATCHER

BY ADAM BLADE

ORCHARD

WAR IS COMING TO THE DELTA QUADRANT!

For too long I have hidden in exile, watching as Gustados, the greatest of all civilisations, becomes weak.

I have swum amongst the Merryn of Sumara in disguise as one of them, and stolen their secrets. I have walked into Aquora, Arctiria, Verdula and Gustados, invisible to any around me. Now I know how to destroy them.

Deception is the greatest weapon. With it I will make the so-called Delta Quadrant Alliance tear itself apart! And in its place the Empire of Gustados will rise, with me as its leader – Kade, the Lord of Illusion!

CHAPTER ONE

PEACE

Max's stomach fizzed with excitement as he swam through clear waters, making one final check on his father's latest construction. It was a giant, air-filled plexiglass dome, right at the heart of the Merryn city of Sumara. Max ran his eyes slowly over each hexagonal panel, looking for cracks, or the slightest trickle of bubbles. Through the plexiglass inside the dome, he could see black-clad Aquoran technicians scurrying about like insects.

"No holes, Max!" Rivet, Max's dogbot, barked from just ahead.

"Just as well!" Lia said. The Merryn princess frowned at the giant structure from the back of her swordfish, Spike. "I can't believe our guests are about to arrive and we're still checking for leaks!"

Max grinned. "Dad's just being extra cautious. We've been all over the dome a

hundred times. And it's made using the latest tech!"

"Hmm," Lia said, "maybe that's what's worrying me." Then she smiled. "Anyway, I can't wait for the ceremony to start!"

Max felt a swell of pride as he ran his eyes over the dome. Without his father's technical skills, Sumara's first deep-sea peace conference would never have been possible.

The sound of chatter and laughter drifted up to them, along with the salty tang of seaweed cakes and festive treats.

Max turned away from the dome and gazed down over Sumara's broad main street, Treaty Avenue. The wide street ran from Treaty Square, straight through the dome, then out the other side, and on to Lia's father's palace. Glowing spheres mounted on coral pillars bathed the avenue in silver light. Merryn of all ages lined the approach to the dome, pressed tightly together, wearing their best beaded tunics. Max could see children and babies on their parents' shoulders waving bright flags.

"It looks like everyone in Sumara's turned out to greet their guests!" Max said.

Lia nodded. "And we couldn't have hoped for better weather." The current stirred her long silver hair, making it shimmer in the soft glow filtering from the dome. The water was crystal clear, with no silt to muddy the view of the surrounding coral towers of Sumara.

"True," Max said. "Which means they should be on time." He lifted his eyes to scan the ocean beyond the city. "In fact – I think that's the first of them arriving now!"

A narrow submarine barge, faceted to shine like a diamond, was gliding slowly towards Sumara, reflecting the lights and colours of the underwater city.

"Pretty boat, Max!" Rivet barked. A chorus of cheers went up from the crowd as the gleaming barge reached Treaty Avenue, then inched towards the docks on the side of the dome.

"That must be the Arctirians," Lia said. "I can't imagine anyone else having the time to keep a sub that clean!"

Max nodded. He and Lia had crossed paths

with the tall, beauty-obsessed Arctirians before. "I hope their ambassadors have better manners than the last Arctirians we met," Max said. "They told us we were ugly, remember? Hey – look!" Max felt a tingle of excitement as he spotted a formidable black and red battle sub behind the mirrored barge. "That's the *Sea Hammer* from back home in Aquora! Councillor Glenon will be on board."

The Arctirian barge slid smoothly into one of the four docks attached to the outside wall of the dome. Through the plexiglass, Max could see a group of Aquoran guards waiting inside next to the Arch of Peace, decked out in full military black and red. The docking stations led through airlocks, straight to the historic arch. All guests would pass under the arch on their way to watch King Salinus sign the Delta Accord, a symbol of the five races of the Delta Quadrant – Aquorans, Sumarans, Arctirians, Verdulans and Gustadians – all finally coming together in peace.

A tall, slim humanoid with a straight back and glowing blue skin emerged from the airlock into the dome. The Arctirian glanced around with a look of pained distaste, before dipping gracefully under the Arch of Peace and into the central arena. More slender Arctirians followed.

Max heard a splash, and turned to see a nut-shaped wooden pod, decorated with wild swirls of red and yellow paint, plunge from the surface, and sink into place behind the Aquoran sub. From the colourful artwork, Max knew the vessel belonged to the monkey-like Verdulan people. *Right on time, which just leaves the Gustadians to arrive…*

"Lia – the ceremony will start soon," Max

said. "I'm going inside to see if Dad needs any help."

"I'll meet you later," Lia said. "I want to watch the procession. Come on, Spike!" Lia and Spike swooped towards the Merryn crowd, who were greeting the Verdulan pod with more cheers.

Max swam down over the side of the dome, towards the seabed, with Rivet. Hydrofilters glowed at intervals around the base of the dome – air and water force-fields designed to let Merryn with facemasks into the dome. Max ducked through the nearest portal, feeling a prickling sensation all over his body. When he stepped inside, his wetsuit and hair were dry. He gazed along Treaty Avenue, past rows of seats on either side, towards the grand platform at the far end.

Max spotted his father tinkering with sound equipment on the stage. King Salinus stood with him, wearing his robes of state. Behind them, a semicircle of empty chairs waited for the quadrant's leaders.

"Everything looks good outside, Dad," Max said, into his headset. "Do you need any help?"

Callum looked up and smiled. "Thanks, Max," he said, "but we're good to go."

The dome was quickly filling with Merryn spectators, filing through the hydrofilters. Each wore an Amphibio mask, allowing them to breathe the air inside the dome. Aquorans and Verdulans streamed from the airlocks through the Arch of Peace. The Arctirians stood in a stiff-backed huddle nearby.

"I simply can't bear all these gaudy lights!" Max heard one say, glancing around at the golden orbs hanging from the dome's ceiling.

"I know," another said, his melodic voice sharp with scorn. "Did you see all those clashing corals out there? I'm going to have a headache for a week."

Max sighed. *Don't they ever stop moaning?*

"And as for his vulgarness, that Gustadian General Phero, well!" A third Arctirian rolled his beautiful, ice-blue eyes. "You'd think even he would have better manners than to arrive late. I really don't know why we're standing for it!"

"Oh, dear goodness!" another said, shielding his eyes from a Verdulan woman dressed in a pink dress and leggings. The Verdulan was shimmying up a metal pole into one of the crow's-nests Max's father had built for the jungle people.

Max turned to scan the dome. The rows of seats were filling fast, and brightly clad Verdulans peered down from the raised crow's-nests above. He spoke into his headset. "Lia, is there any sign of the Gustadian delegation? The Arctirians are grumbling."

Lia growled. "That lot were born grumbling," she said. "Hang on, I'll take a look. Wait – there's a grey sub in the distance. That must be the Gustadians."

"Great!" Max said. "I'll let everyone know!" He switched his comms set to loud speaker, sending an electric shriek of feedback around the dome. The Arctirians clapped their hands over their ears, while the Verdulans let out loud answering screeches.

Once the noise had died down, Max cleared his throat. "Sorry for the delay, everyone. The Gustadians will arrive shortly. Please make yourself comfortable." Max's words echoed back to him in each of the languages of the quadrant from a huge speaker on the stage.

Before long, Max heard a hum as the final airlock into the dome slid open, and General Phero emerged through the Arch of Peace. The Gustadian leader stood as tall and imposing as ever, a long black cape draped over his broad shoulders. His ash-grey face and black eyes were stern as he scanned the crowd.

"Please be seated!" Callum's voice echoed around the dome. "It's time to welcome the leaders of the Delta Quadrant!"

Merryn ushers wearing coral armour steered the Treaty members into a procession heading along Treaty Avenue, towards the dais where Callum and King Salinus waited.

"Let's go, Riv!" Max said, hurrying towards the stage. He took the steps two at a time and slipped into place beside his father, just as Lia arrived, out of breath.

"I left Spike outside to play with some friends," she murmured.

A slow fanfare started up from an Aquoran band at the back of the stage, and the Treaty members filed forwards.

The Arctirians were first to be greeted. Their cool fingers barely touched Max's as he offered his hand. Next came Councillor Glenon. The old man's eyes crinkled into a warm smile as he squeezed Max's outstretched hand. The Verdulan leader, Naybor, shuffled forwards next, snatching up Max's hand in a sinewy grip, his monkey-like mouth spread into a grin.

Finally, General Phero approached. Max stuck out his hand. "Good to see you again, sir!" he said.

The general frowned. "Do I know you?" he asked. The tall guard at his side whispered something in Gustadian, and the general's lipless mouth twitched into a polite smile. "Of course!" he said, nodding. "Max. Always a pleasure."

As Phero moved on, Lia raised an eyebrow. "You'd have thought he'd remember the people who saved his city from a giant snake," she said.

Max watched the Gustadian leader take his seat. "Maybe he's ill? he said.

King Salinus stepped towards the microphone at the front of the stage and Callum slipped into his seat beside

Councillor Glenon. Max and Lia hurried down the steps into their own front-row benches, ready to listen to the king's speech. Rivet sank to the ground at Max's feet, his nose on his paws. All around them, the low murmur of chatter mingled with the hum of the air recycling system.

Suddenly Max felt Rivet stir. The dogbot's ears pricked. Then he shot to his feet and started barking.

"Shhh, Riv!" Max whispered.

"Something bad, Max!" Rivet barked, his tail stuck straight out behind him and his nose pointed towards the stage. King Salinus waited, frowning in Max and Rivet's direction.

"Rivet, sit down!" Max hissed.

But instead, Rivet leapt up and dived towards the stage. He stopped before the platform, his whole body quivering with agitation. A low growl rumbled in his throat.

Max raced to Rivet's side, shocked gasps and amused sniggers echoing around him. "What is it, Riv?"

"Down there, Max! Look!" Rivet barked. Max followed the line of the dogbot's muzzle. In the shadows beneath the stage, he saw something that turned his blood cold. The faintest flash of red light, illuminating a mass of silvery wires.

Max had helped his father make every bit of tech for the event. This wasn't one of their inventions. It was a bomb. And it was strapped to the stage directly beneath every leader in the quadrant.

CHAPTER TWO

GLUE BOMB

Adrenaline raced through Max's veins as he stared at the lethal device. Who would do something so evil?

"What is it, Max?" Callum's voice spoke into his headset.

"A bomb," Max hissed.

From the shadows beneath the stage, he could hear a faint *tick, tick* as the bomb timer counted down. Red digits on the screen glowed bright in the darkness: twenty-one seconds. Twenty and counting. Max's mouth went dry and his skin prickled with sweat.

"No time to defuse it!" he told his father. "Get everyone out, now!"

"Evacuate the dome at once!" Max's father announced.

Guests scrambled to their feet. Aquoran and Merryn guards raced to the end of each row of seats, directing the Merryn to the hydrofilters, and the breathers towards the Arch of Peace.

Naybor leapt from the stage, closely followed by Councillor Glenon and the other leaders, as well as Callum, Lia and the king. All were soon lost in a sea of pushing, shoving bodies clawing their way along Treaty Avenue towards the Arch of Peace.

Max dived into the scrum with Rivet at his heels. Long-armed Verdulans swarmed overhead, using the lighting hanging from the top of the dome. A tall Gustadian shoved past, barging Max into the path of a slender Arctirian, who tutted and elbowed him out of the way. Max scrambled on towards a huge knot of terrified people pressing to get out of the dome.

BOOM!

Max was bowled over by the force of the blast. Screams echoed around him, and bent bits of metal clattered down on every side. Acrid smoke caught in his throat, making him wheeze. When the sound of falling debris finally stopped, Max scrambled up. Beside him, an Arctirian brushed the dust from his blue skin, and Max could see Lia helping her father up. Callum stood nearby, frowning at the scene, his dark hair grey with soot. The stage was a wreck of twisted metal and wood, with a smoking hole through the centre. Debris and fallen seats littered the dome, all covered in some sort of smouldering goo.

But Max couldn't see anyone trapped under the wreckage. They had cleared the blast zone in time!

"Big bang, Max!" Rivet barked, bounding towards Max.

As if they had been waiting for Rivet's voice to break the silence, the crowd of people around the arch all started talking at once. Angry and frightened shouts in five languages filled the dome.

King Salinus held up a hand. "Please remain calm!" he called.

Callum turned to Max. "You and Lia inspect the damage. The king and I will organise the evacuation." He and Salinus strode towards the Arch of Peace.

"Max! Look!" Lia called, her voice high and urgent. Max turned to see her staring at something on the wall of the dome – a blob of sizzling goo. Max ran his eyes over the panels above the wreck of the stage, and spotted more patches of fizzing slime. His stomach twisted with dread.

"Dad!" he said into his headset. "We have to get masks on the air breathers! The bomb released acid and it's burning through the plexiglass! The dome's going to flood!"

"I hear you, Max," Callum said calmly. Max looked to see his father duck behind one of the columns of the Arch of Peace. When he reappeared he was carrying a box they had stowed in one of the airlocks for just such an emergency. Callum drew out a mask and thrust it towards Councillor Glenon. The councillor strapped it on, then grabbed more from the box and started to hand them out.

"All air-breathing guests, please secure a mask over your nose and mouth," Callum announced. In an instant, he and Councillor Glenon were surrounded by pushing bodies and grasping fingers.

"We'd better help," Lia said, glancing at a fizzing section of wall. "I don't think we've got long."

Max grabbed an armful of masks from his father and plunged into the heaving chaos of bodies, squeezing between broad-shouldered Gustadians and dodging hairy Verdulan elbows.

There was a tricky moment when Max

shoved a mask into the slender fingers of the Arctirian ambassador, only to find it quickly handed back.

"I can't wear that!" the man said with a frown. "It won't suit me at all!"

"Have it your own way," Max said. "You can leave it off if you think drowning will suit you better!" He pointed to a bulging section of ceiling. Water oozed through a crack, drizzling into the dome. The tall man sniffed, but took the mask and fixed it over his face.

A deafening roar filled the dome as part of the ceiling gave way and a torrent of water crashed through. The lights sparked out, plunging the dome into half-darkness. Max glanced up through the gloom to see more panels collapsing. Water swirled across the floor, pouring in on every side.

"Dad, what shall Lia and I do to help?"

Max asked through his headset.

"Find General Phero," Callum answered. "He's not in the Gustadian sub, and none of his bodyguards can find him."

"Leave it to us, Dad," Max said. He turned to Rivet. "Riv, stay here and help Callum. Lia and I have to find General Phero."

"Yes, Max!" Rivet barked.

Lia scanned the dome. "Could Phero have been swept through one of the hydrofilters by the blast?" she asked.

Max felt a jab of fear. "If he was, we'd better find him before he drowns!"

Max and Lia ducked beneath the rising water and swam through a shimmering portal.

Outside, the festive lights on Treaty Avenue looked out of place. Max saw a wide-eyed Merryn mother desperately trying to calm a pair of toddlers, while a father turned his sniffling brood towards home. Merryn guards swam backwards and forwards above the horror-struck crowd, bringing new panels of plexiglass and trying to shore up the dome.

Max and Lia swum upwards for a better view. A steady current whooshed past them as water gushed through holes in the dome and bubbles streamed out. Max glanced towards the palace.

A broad figure, taller than any Merryn and clad in a flowing black cape, was swimming over the palace gardens towards the tower that housed the king's chambers.

"That has to be General Phero," Lia said. "But what's he doing?"

"I don't know," Max said, frowning, "but he clearly isn't drowning. We'd better follow him. Whoever planted that bomb is still on the loose. Phero could be in serious danger."

Max and Lia swam away from the dome and through the palace gardens, flitting between statues and fronds of kelp. The figure ahead swam with strong, steady strokes until he reached the entrance to the king's chambers. There, he parted a curtain of weed and slipped inside.

"Where are the guards?" Max asked.

"Good question," Lia said. "Helping with the evacuation, I hope."

They followed the intruder into a picture-lined passageway, just in time to see a figure dart through the archway at the end in a swirl of glittering robes.

Lia gasped. Max stopped, frowning in confusion. The person he'd seen swim into the palace had definitely looked like a Gustadian. But the figure he'd seen pass through the archway hadn't been the black-clad General Phero at all. Instead, it had looked like King Salinus, dressed in his robes of state. *But that's impossible!*

CHAPTER THREE

IMPOSTER ALERT

"What's going on?" Max hissed. "Isn't the king helping evacuate the dome?"

Lia swallowed and nodded. "That can't have been my father. Someone's impersonating him and heading straight for his private rooms!"

"Someone that can switch disguise in an instant," Max said. "It could be our bomber. We have to stop him!"

Max and Lia raced after the intruder, through the curtained archway into King Salinus's dressing room. Tunics and robes hung from rows of bone pegs on the walls. Max caught a flicker of movement to his right, but when he looked, he saw only his own pale face reflected in a slab of mica. They crossed the room and ducked through a second archway into the king's bed chamber. His wide clamshell bed dominated the room, with a gilt dressing table to one side. The intruder stood there, his back to Max and Lia, peering into a scallop-shell box.

"Right! That's it!" Lia shouted, swooping across the room. "Get your hands off my mother's jewellery!"

The intruder spun around. The king's features were twisted with fury as he snatched a golden ring with a branching coral stone from the shell, then threw the box at Lia.

Lia dodged. "Give that ring back!" she cried, aiming a high kick at the figure who looked like her father. The intruder dodged aside as quickly as a snake, caught Lia's foot and thrust her away. He shoved the ring into his pocket, and dived for the exit. Max lunged, cutting off his escape, then swung his fist at the imposter's chest. His hand connected with something hard but invisble, inches from the man's embroidered tunic. The shock sent Max reeling back, gripping his fist. As the visitor elbowed past, Max snatched for the edge of his cloak, but his fingers passed through the billowing material as if it wasn't there. *What's going on?*

Lia grabbed the imposter's shoulder. Max saw a shimmer of movement in the water around her fingers, almost like electrical static, before the man turned and kicked her in the chest, sending her tumbling across the room. *He's wearing a holographic disguise! But who is he?*

As Lia righted herself, Max saw the impostor transform before his eyes. The king's stern eyes and sharp nose morphed

into a younger Merryn face with smooth features. The embroidered robed shimmered and became a simple green shift. Then the stranger touched a button on a device at his wrist and vanished.

A flicker of movement from the corner of Max's eye caught his attention, and he spun around to see the man reappear on the other side of the room, beneath the window. *What? He can teleport too?* The man's eyes narrowed and his lips spread into a cruel smile. He lifted a pistol with a bulbous chamber at the back and aimed it at Max.

A stream of thick grey liquid spurted from the gun, straight towards Max's chest.

Boof! Lia cannoned into Max, knocking him away from the blast. A haze of bubbles filled the room, pouring from a hole in the wall where the liquid had struck. Max and Lia coughed, their eyes streaming. They scrambled up and peered through the murky water just in time to see the stranger dive through the bedroom window.

Still wheezing, Max raced past the king's bed to the window and looked out over the palace gardens towards the dome. The water was empty, apart from a few Merryn guards in the distance, carrying sheets of plexiglass. The figure had vanished.

"This is hopeless!" Max said, as Lia arrived at his side. "How can we possibly find a man that can teleport and change shape?"

"I don't know," Lia said. "But we're going to have to. That goo he fired at you is way too much like the stuff dissolving the dome to be a coincidence."

"But surely no one would try to blow up all the Delta Quadrant leaders just to steal a ring. It doesn't make sense!" Max gazed out at the plexiglass dome. The roof was bowing inwards now. It looked like a boiled egg that had been hit by a spoon. Max could see Merryn and Aquorans with facemasks side by side, trying to fix panels over dozens of holes still streaming with bubbles. The inside was more than half filled with water and floating rubble.

Then, suddenly, like a house of cards caught by a sigh of wind, the dome collapsed into a tumble of whirling debris, sending up a great plume of glittering bubbles.

"No!" Max's stomach clenched in horror as he thought of all the people still inside. Then he felt an even sharper stab of fear. "Dad!"

CHAPTER FOUR

A CONFERENCE IN RUINS

Max dived through the window and towards the dome, terror squeezing his chest. The structure lay in ruins – a pile of transparent hexagons, like the discarded skin of a giant snake. Once the bubbles had cleared, Max could see the Merryn and Aquoran engineers gazing down from above, frozen with shock, still holding sheets of plexiglass.

Max felt sick. As Lia arrived at his side, he tapped the code for his father's comms system into his headset. "Dad! Are you okay?"

A warm wave of relief rushed over him as his headset crackled, and his father's voice came through. "Alive and well, Max," Callum said. "We evacuated the dome just in time. We're holding a meeting on the *Sea Hammer* with the leaders – all except General Phero. Did you find him?"

"Sort of," Max said. "I'm headed your way.

I'll explain when we get there."

o o o

Max and Lia found the mess-hall of the *Sea Hammer* crowded, noisy and thrumming with tension. The quadrant leaders and their guards were crammed into the small space, seated at fixed, metal tables only ever designed for Aquorans. The Arctirians were squashed

around one table with their long legs tucked up under their chins, sipping kelp juice with obvious distaste. The Verdulans stood on their table, chattering loudly, their tattooed faces creased with anger as they gestured at the other delegates. Naybor was nodding, patting the air placatingly, but Max could see that his advisers were anything but calm.

The Gustadians looked the least comfortable of all. They stood huddled, their huge eyes downcast as they muttered to each other. Councillor Glenon was with them.

"We're waiting for word of General Phero even now..." he said, then he spotted Max. "Ah! Max! What news do you have?"

"Indeed!" the Arctirian ambassador shouted. "What's become of the treacherous assassin? I'd imagine he's far from here after his attempt to destroy us all with his glue bomb. Only a Gustadian could use such a vulgar weapon."

The Verdulans on their table nearby nodded vigorously.

General Phero's personal guard lifted his hand. "Hey!" he said, his guttural voice echoing through a translator crystal. "How do we know one of *you* didn't plant the bomb to frame us?"

Callum stood with King Salinus and Rivet near a serving hatch. "We must work together," he said, calmly. "Whoever is responsible for this act of terror will have done it to create conflict. We must not give them that satisfaction. This is a peace conference, after all."

The room quietened a little, but Max noticed that the delegates were still eyeing each other suspiciously. Callum beckoned Max and Lia over. Councillor Glenon joined them, and Rivet nosed his way to Max's feet.

"Phew!" Callum wiped a film of sweat from his brow. "Max, please tell me you've found the general." He ran his eyes around the room, keeping his voice low. "I don't know how long we can keep this lot from coming to blows."

King Salinus nodded gravely, his nose and mouth hidden behind an Amphibio mask. "We can't allow the first Sumaran peace conference to end in war."

"It's not good news," Max said. "We thought our terrorist was Phero, and followed him to the palace. But then we lost him. We're not *sure* he was Phero, anyway. He had some advanced tech that allowed him to teleport across the room and to disguise himself." Callum took a sharp breath, and Max nodded. "I have no idea how he did it. He even impersonated King Salinus. And he used a weapon that fired the same sort of glue as the bomb."

Callum rubbed the stubble on his chin. "I've never heard of technology that can teleport a whole person," he said, "let alone allow them to change shape. We can't let this get out. If people find out there might be a high-tech assassin in our midst, there'll be chaos."

Lia put her hand on her father's. "There's more," she said. "The impostor stole one of Mother's rings. The one with the branching coral tree."

King Salinus lifted his webbed hand to rest on his daughter's shoulder. "That is sad news," he said. "That ring was your mother's favourite. According to ancient legend, it belonged to Addulis himself, and had the power to summon four guardians from Deepholm Temple to protect Sumara in its time of need." Salinus sighed, and let his hand drop. "Sadly, Deepholm Temple was destroyed in a seaquake decades ago."

Max frowned. "The question is, why would a bomber with tech powerful enough to teleport and change shape steal a bit of old jewellery?"

"Hey!" Lia jabbed Max in the ribs. "That's my mum's ring you're talking about!"

Max winced. "Sorry. I know it's important to you. But you must see what I mean?"

Lia's scowl faded and she sighed. "I suppose it doesn't make much sense. Unless the bomber thinks the legend about the temple guardians is true."

King Salinus let out a gruff laugh. "I wish it were. Ancient magical defenders would be a great help to Sumara right now. The peace conference is a shambles!"

"I think the only way to save it is to bring our shape-shifting bomber to trial," Callum said. "But he could be miles away by now. I'll have to stay here and make sure things don't get out of hand…" Callum paused and flinched as an Arctirian aimed a spray of perfume at the Verdulan table. A slender female Verdulan with bright tattoos on her wiry arms leaned over and let out a rumbling belch in response. "Or any *more* out of hand," Callum said. His face went suddenly grave. "Max – it's a dangerous mission and I wouldn't send you if I had a choice, but I'm trusting you to find that bomber. It's our only chance." Then he smiled, as if he'd remembered something. "There's something for you in the docking bay that you might find useful on your Quest."

"I'm coming too!" Lia piped up. "I am not letting some sneaking thief keep my mum's ring. I've got little enough to remember her by. I say we try Deepholm first."

Salinus smiled sadly. "I think you're right, Lia. Your mother would be proud of you. She was a brave woman and you are like her in so many ways."

"Rivet come too, Max!" Rivet barked. "Rivet find baddy!"

Lia laughed. "Of course we wouldn't leave

you behind, Rivet, or Spike. Who else would help sniff out our thief?"

"Let's go, then," Max said.

They said goodbye to Callum and King Salinus, then clattered down some metal stairs. Max swiped his pass to open a pair of airtight sliding doors, and Lia and Rivet followed him into the docking bay.

Military aquabikes lined the walls, but they weren't new or exciting. The transparent sphere that sat in the middle of the room was, though.

"Whoa! An aquasphere!" Max breathed. "That is the coolest bit of tech ever!"

Lia let out a giggle. "That thing?" she said. "It looks like a giant bubble! There's a reason fish aren't generally round, you know. It's not exactly streamlined."

Max ran a hand over the sphere. The double-thickness plexiglass ball was the size of a small hovercar, with chrome twin blasters on either

side and multiple circular thrusters built into
its walls. Through the plexiglass, Max could
see a padded cockpit with holoscreens and a
steering lever studded with buttons.

"Bubbles can move pretty fast," Max said.
"Dad must have made it from leftovers from
the dome. It's perfect for a Sea Quest!"

"If you say so," Lia said. Then she grinned.
"So, what are we waiting for?"

CHAPTER FIVE

SHADOWREACH

Max frowned into the inky water ahead, his fists tight on the aquasphere's steering lever as they raced onwards. Below, the seabed rose and fell in pools of light cast by his headlamps – an endless plane of craggy rock, mottled with pale sea moss.

"Dark, Max!" Rivet barked.

"It'll get darker still, Riv," Lia said, her voice echoing through the aquasphere's speakers. They had left Sumara behind long ago. Lia rode Spike alongside the sphere, her coral spear tucked under one arm, her face ghostly in the gloom. "We're getting close to Shadowreach," she said. "It's one of the deepest sea trenches in Nemos. The legends say the Deepholm Temple was constructed inside. But we'll be lucky to find anything left of it. As my dad said, the whole site was swallowed by a seaquake decades ago."

"There has to be something left," Max said, "or, at least, that shape-shifter must think so."

"Whatever he thinks, I'm not letting him get away with my mother's ring," Lia said. "He's going to stand trial before my father!"

"Too right," Max said. "Unless we get answers about the bombing soon, this will be the first peace conference in history to trigger a war."

Lia groaned. "Don't remind me." She pointed past a shoal of jellyfish pulsing with electric light. "Do you see it?" she asked.

Max followed the line of her finger. In the distance, the rocky seabed dropped away over a jagged ledge, plunging into blackness. A vast chasm stretched away as far as Max's headlamps reached in either direction, yawning darkly. As they drew nearer, Max swung his headlamps down its sides, but apart from the fleeting forms of pale, toothy fish, the sharp beams of light met nothing.

"Big hole, Max!" Rivet barked, his red eyes bright points in the gloom.

Max nodded. He glanced at Lia and saw that she was biting her lip. Spike's body shone like silver in the faint light from the sphere as the swordfish gazed fearfully into the chasm. "Where do we start?" Max asked.

Lia scanned the edge of the trench and shook her head. "I wish I knew."

Suddenly, Spike let out a sharp warning click and Rivet growled.

Five black triangular shapes, flat and sharp like arrow heads, broke away from the deeper blackness below and shot up towards Max and Lia in a tight V formation. Max gripped his steering lever.

What are they? Some sort of fish? The blade-like objects swooped close. Each let out a volley of energy bolts, before dancing away.

"Enemy fire! The shape-shifter must have got here before us!" Max cried, tugging the steering lever. His stomach flipped as the aquasphere lurched between the sizzling energy beams. *Whoa! This thing is fast!*

Spike and Lia zipped through the hail of fizzing energy bolts. Max dodged right and left, red beams streaking past the aquasphere's plexiglass walls.

Two can play at this game! Max thought, scanning his dashboard. *Twin turbo-blasters! Thanks, Dad!* Max spun around and swerved

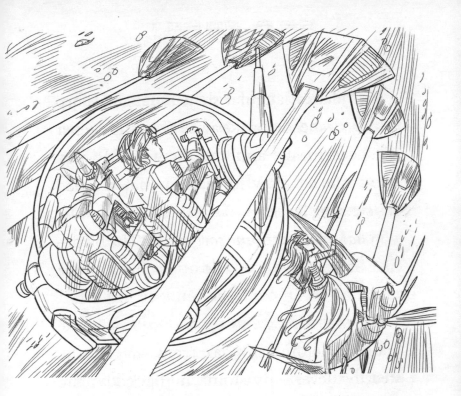

after the enemy craft, slamming between blazing energy bolts until he had a sub in his sights. He pressed fire, and the wing of the craft flared white where his twin blasts hit. *Yes!* The arrow-shaped vessel plunged into a spin. Just before it smashed into the seabed, Max saw something shiny drop from its base. A moment later a flare of orange obscured his view as the craft burst into flames.

Max glanced up to see the four remaining subs banking steeply towards Lia and Spike. Lia swerved up to meet them, lifting her spear. She smashed it hard into the wing of the leading craft. The sub lurched into a nosedive, spinning out of control. This time, Max clearly saw another silvery pod eject, before the vessel plunged into the rocky seabed, exploding into shiny black shards. The other three enemy subs knifed after it, then swooped around back towards Max. Max gripped his blaster controls, his veins fizzing with adrenaline. *Bam!* He sent another energy burst towards the triangular subs. The sleek craft zigzagged through his energy beams. *Missed!*

"Max!" Lia cried, as she and Spike swam alongside the sphere. "Don't get too close, those wings are as sharp as blades. They'd slice right through your aquasphere."

"Not to mention our skin!" Max said. "Look out!" The subs dived towards them in another tight, deadly V.

"Into the canyon!" Max cried. He raced towards the crevasse, the water all around him ablaze with red energy bolts. He glanced back to see the vessels hot on his tail, still firing round after round.

Lia and Spike streaked beside him. Red light filled the aquasphere, and the sound of sizzling blaster fire sent a shiver down Max's spine. They dived into shadow, hugging tight to the craggy wall.

Ahead, outlined in the main beams of the aquasphere, Max saw the dark forms of the three enemy craft overshoot them, going too fast to slow down, speeding on towards the far wall of the trench. Shiny pods dropped from the crafts into blackness. The next instant, the blade-shaped vessels careered into the rocky wall.

Crunch! Crash! Thud! They crumpled, sending twisted metal tumbling into the shadows below.

"Baddies all gone!" Rivet barked.

"We outmanoeuvred them!" Lia said, grinning.

"So maybe my bubble craft isn't such a

bad design after all?" Max said.

Lia shrugged, but then she smiled. "I guess you're right. And at least now we know we're in the right place. Those craft must have something to do with our mystery bomber. Whoever he is…"

Max shook his head. "I've never seen craft like that before. They were so fast!"

"You can say that again!" Lia said. "Hey, look at that damage down there!"

Max shone his main beams towards the far side of the trench. Parallel gouges had been scored through the rock. "That's not natural," Max said. "Let's take a closer look."

They crossed the trench and Max let the aquasphere sink slowly towards the scarred rock. As they drifted closer, Max could see how sharp blades had broken the ancient corals, smashing branches from some and uprooting others completely.

They descended further, passing spindly white crabs picking their way over the damaged rock.

Finally, they reached the edge of a huge hole torn into the canyon wall. Max angled his beams inside, but could see nothing but smooth walls, funnelling into darkness.

"Max, turn off the lights a moment," Lia said, "I think I saw something."

Max flicked the switch, plunging them into semi-darkness. Deep in the far reaches of the tunnel, he spotted a glimmer of blue light.

"Something in there, Max," Rivet said, his electronic voice low and his red eyes staring into the shadows.

Spike let out a mournful clack.

"I know," Lia said, stroking her swordfish's side. "It's scary. But we have to keep going."

The faint light shone from a narrow fissure between two boulders. The crack looked just big enough for Lia and Spike to squeeze through, but too small for the aquasphere.

"I guess this is where we get off, Riv," Max said. He hit the release for the aquasphere's lid, and he and Rivet swam out. Spike eyed the glowing gap between the rocks nervously as Lia slid from his back.

"You stay here and guard the aquasphere, Spike," she said. "We don't know how big the space is in there, and I don't want you getting stuck!" Spike lifted his head and let out a grateful chirp.

Max sized up the gap, his stomach heavy with dread. There could be wolfsharks or Robobeasts, or anything through there... And what if we get stuck? But if they wanted to prevent a war, they had to go inside. Max swallowed hard, then swam forward and ducked between the two boulders.

CHAPTER SIX

DEEPHOLM TEMPLE

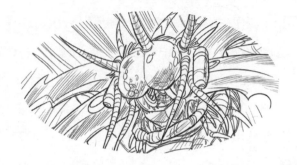

Max squeezed between the closely piled rocks. Blue light glared in his eyes, and he could hear Rivet and Lia scrabbling through the cleft behind him. The rock pressed close about him until he felt he could hardly breathe. Finally, the passageway opened up, and Max kicked out into a vast chamber lit by bright blue light. He gasped, drawing a deep breath of cold water over his gills, half in relief, half in wonder.

"Oh!" Lia exclaimed behind him. They were in a huge underwater temple, carved from rock, and lit by electric blue floodlights bolted to the ceiling.

Pale columns of stone, half covered in sea moss, rose from the floor up to a vaulted ceiling far above. More columns stretched away ahead and to either side, creating a grid of open squares. Statues and altars decorated the square spaces, and a few contained metal

workbenches, riveted together, alongside piles of components and power tools. Cracks ran across the floor and chunks of ceiling and broken pillars lay scattered everywhere. In amongst the debris, cables looped from the floodlights to rows of sockets on the floor.

"Deepholm Temple!" Lia said.

"And it looks like someone's set up a lab inside it!" Max said. As he spoke, he felt the water stir behind him, and heard a hiss, like

a snake – or like the sharp intake of water through a breathing mask. He spun around, but could see nothing. Then he noticed silt, disturbed from the mosaic floor, swirling in a strange current, like a heat haze.

"Riv, shine your beams over there," Max said, pointing. At first, all he could see was pale stone, cracked and worn by time, but as he looked harder, he noticed the shimmering outline of a tall humanoid. Max grabbed for his hyperblade just as a blaster appeared in front of the hidden being, aimed at Max's chest.

With a swish, four more blasters appeared, floating in the water, all pointed his way. *The pilots of those subs!* Max realised.

"Take cover!" he cried, diving behind a column as five energy bullets sizzled towards him. Lia and Rivet swooped to his side. Max drew his blaster and peered out from behind a pillar, aiming at the wall above a floating weapon. *Bam!* His energy blast hit something metallic and flared brightly. As the light faded, Max caught a glimpse of a tall, armour-clad figure with the greyish skin and flat nose of a Gustadian. The man lifted his blaster and Max ducked back out of sight.

"Gustadians!" Lia said.

"And they've got the same stealth-suit technology as our thief," Max said.

"Danger, Max!" Rivet barked, staring towards an altar on their left. Max turned to see another blaster floating before it, aimed at his head.

"Come on!" Lia cried, grabbing Max's arm and tugging him after her. "It's five blasters to one. We don't stand a chance!"

Max, Lia and Rivet fled, energy blasts ricochetting off the stone all around them. They ducked between pillars and dived over work benches, racing through the temple. Harsh blue light glared down from the ceiling, casting dark shadows into every corner. Max scanned the cluttered space, his scalp prickling with fear, but could see nothing amongst the carved pillars except swaying sea moss.

Rivet led them on through the complex, listening and sniffing, ducking behind columns and statues as they went. At last they reached a magnificent arch, carved with sea snakes and fish.

They swam through the arch into a room very different from the complex they had left, lit by softly glowing white lights. It was vast, with giant square plinths at each of its four corners. Three stood empty, while the fourth housed a towering S-shaped statue. It looked like a giant, flat, segmented worm, with hundreds of triangular legs running down

each side. The statue had a blunt head with
a pair of sharp-toothed prongs sprouting
at right angles from each side of its round,
gaping mouth. Patches of weed had been
scraped away from the statue's body to make
room for gleaming metal plates.

Pow! An energy blast struck the floor at Max's feet.

"Hide, Max!" Rivet barked. Max, Lia and Rivet ducked behind the nearest empty plinth. Mounds of pale, shell-like rubble littered the ground. It crunched under Max's boots as he shifted his feet. "Four plinths," Max whispered. "Does that remind you of something?"

Lia nodded. "The four guardians of Deepholm. The ancient Merryn must have carved statues of them. But if that's the case, why has someone been decorating one of the statues with tech, and what happened to the other three?"

"A good question that I shall answer shortly!" a clear, cheerful voice said behind them. At the same moment, Max felt a wave of something heavy and thick hit his side, quickly flowing around his body, gripping his limbs. He tried to turn, but found he could hardly move at all. He was held fast in a thick layer of glue.

"Argh!" Lia cried, struggling against the gunge too.

"Trapped, Max!" Rivet barked.

"Correct," the voice spoke again. "I have something to show you, and I wanted to make sure you stuck about!" The voice had an electronic quality to it that Max recognised. A moment later, the water before Max and Lia flickered, and the speaker appeared.

"General Phero!" Lia said. "So you really *are* a traitor to Delta Quadrant!"

The general smiled, and the water around him shimmered and blurred. Max blinked, and found himself looking at King Salinus. Lia gasped. The Merryn king's features swam and, a moment later, resolved into a new figure – a tall, young Gustadian with skin so pale Max could see the knotted blue veins beneath it. The right side of the man's face, from his smooth white temple all the way to his almost lipless mouth, shone with a coating of cracked, silvery metal that looked as if it had been melted onto his skin. A narrow tube ran from one of his wide flat nostrils, down the side of his face, and disappeared into his neck.

That must let him breathe underwater! Max realised.

The Gustadian's thin lips twitched into a crooked smile, half frozen by the metal that marred his face. He lifted a pale hand, and wiggled his fingers in a mocking wave. Then he turned it over to reveal a golden ring with a huge, branching coral stone.

"That's my mother's!" Lia cried, struggling furiously against the glue that held her.

"Indeed," the man said. "It didn't quite fit, but now that I've adjusted it, it rather suits

me, don't you think?" Lia scowled, her eyes flashing with fury as the man went on. "I'm Kade, by the way. These are my men." He gestured behind him. Five tall Gustadians, wearing black armour and breathing tubes, flickered into view.

"I'm so glad you've come all this way to find me," Kade said to Max and Lia. "It will make it much easier to pay you back for spoiling my plans. I wanted to be rid of all the quadrant leaders at once, you see, but now I'll have to pick them off one by one."

"Bad Gustadian, Max!" Rivet barked.

"That's all a matter of perspective," Kade said, smiling down at the dogbot. "And, of course, it depends on who's left behind to write the history books." He lifted his lopsided smirk to Max. "Nice robot, by the way. So quirky to choose an animal with such limited intellect." Rivet let out a low growl, but Kade ignored him. "I do enjoy making gadgets myself. Although just recently I've come to appreciate the mystical. The old ways have their uses. I'll show you what I mean, if you promise not to go anywhere." The Gustadian flashed Max a twisted grin, then strode towards the fourth plinth. Max watched with growing dread as Kade balled his fist and fitted the pronged coral shape on the ring into a narrow opening on the plinth.

"Max!" Lia said, her voice high with fear. "We have to stop him. He's going to wake the temple guardian!"

Max struggled against the goo covering his body, straining his shoulders and neck to get free, but he couldn't move. He watched in horror as Kade turned his hand, twisting the ring on his knuckle in its slot.

CHAPTER SEVEN

THE GUARDIAN AWAKES

A deafening *CLICK* echoed through the temple. The floor shuddered, sending up swirling eddies of silt. A low boom, like thunder in the mountains, rumbled all around them, growing louder and closer.

The statue on the plinth trembled, dislodging trickles of dust. The trembling grew and cracks appeared all over the statue's surface. Plates of barnacle-encrusted stone tumbled free.

Kade spread his arms wide, grinning up at the beast he had unleashed. His men huddled behind him, their black eyes wide with fear. *CRASH!* More slabs of stone toppled from the giant worm's body. Rivet whimpered, his eyes flashing with alarm; Lia's face was as pale as chalk.

The worm flexed, shaking away the last fragments of stone, revealing a brown segmented body with short, tooth-like legs running down either side. Max tried to swallow the horror building in his throat as the plates of metal bolted along the worm's length tightened with a series of hums and clicks. *Kade's turned the temple guardian into a Robobeast!*

The Robobeast lifted its huge mouth towards the ceiling and let out a deep howl of rage. The sound echoed through the temple, rising in volume, shaking the walls until jagged cracks opened in the rock.

Just as Max thought the temple would collapse, the howl faded, and the worm dived from its platform straight towards one of Kade's armoured men. The man yelped, his fingers scrabbling at the controls on his suit. He hit a switch and vanished in a

shimmering holographic haze. The worm's pincers slammed shut, empty. The creature let out a hiss of rage and turned, its vast, round mouth gaping as it lunged towards Kade. Kade slowly turned his hand, still smiling, and held his ring out. The vast worm froze, as if suddenly turned back to stone. A smooth jewel set below the monster's mouth lit up with a pale blue glow.

"Behold Gort the Deadly Snatcher!" Kade cried.

The stealth-suited Gustadians lifted their fists and punched the water with cheers. At the same moment, a tremendous boom echoed from the ceiling above. The Gustadians' triumphant expressions faltered, and Max felt a stab of fear. He glanced up to see massive cracks tracing their way across the ceiling.

Without Gort's body to hold it up, the temple ceiling was crumbling.

"Danger, Max!" Rivet barked. "Escape!"

Kade turned to Rivet and smiled. "I couldn't have put it better myself," he said. "Men – it's time to leave. We have everything we came for." He held his ring up before the Robobeast once again. "Gort! Take care of our guests!" He waved a dismissive hand at Max and Lia, still stuck tight in their cocoons of glue. The blue stone on Gort's throat pulsed brightly in answer. *The ring controls the beast through that stone!* Max realised. Kade kicked up from the ground and swam for the door, his armoured men following.

Gort turned its vast circular maw towards Max and Lia, the toothed pincers on either side sticking straight out. Five long feelers jutted up from the top of its head, like the prongs of a crown. They swivelled forwards, trembling as they tasted the water.

"It's sensing us," Max hissed. "If we're quiet maybe—"

"Blades, Max!" Rivet's bark cut him off.

So much for staying silent!

Gort's vast head snapped around. Max's whole body jolted with fear as he saw a propeller buried deep in the creature's throat start up with a whine. He felt water rush past him, sucked into the gaping mouth. The monstrous worm dived across the room, snaking straight towards them.

Max heaved and struggled to escape, his

heart thundering like it was about to burst. He could feel the trembling of Rivet's metal body through the glue that bound them together. Lia's eyes were huge and bright in the gloom.

Suddenly, Max felt the water ripple, and a soft chattering from behind them filled him with hope. Something tugged at the glue around his arms, and suddenly they were free. Max glanced around to see Spike, sawing at the glue with his sword, freeing Lia and Rivet.

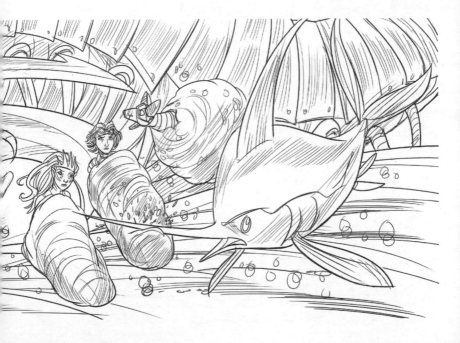

Gort's vast head cannoned closer, its round mouth open wide, filled with deadly spinning blades.

Max lifted his blaster and sent a red energy blast sizzling towards the worm. It struck armour just below the monster's open mouth. The creature recoiled, but then rose up, unharmed. The metal blades in its

mouth whirred and its blunt head struck out once more. Lia finally struggled free of the goo and leapt onto Spike's back. Spike's sword snickered right and left, and suddenly Max could move his legs. *I'm free!* He and Rivet dived after Spike, out of range of the Robobeast.

CRUNCH! The worm's head struck right where they had been huddled just a moment before, sending up a tornado of whirling stones. Max flung up his arms to shield his face. Chunks of rock shot through the water all around, and Max heard a metallic thunk and a yelp as one bounced off Rivet. The worm reared up and howled. The chamber juddered and more cracks appeared in the ceiling. *The whole place is going to collapse!* Max swallowed hard, and pointed his blaster up through the falling debris, right above Gort's open mouth. *I hope this works!* Max gritted his teeth, and pulled the trigger.

BOOM! A great section of vaulted ceiling tumbled down in a cascade of silt and shattered rock. A curved piece of stone smashed down onto Gort's neck like a yoke, pinning the Robobeast to the ground. It writhed, its pincers opening and shutting uselessly.

"Good thinking, Max!" Lia said. "Now, let's go!" She and Spike sped from the room.

Max grabbed Rivet's back. "Go, boy!" he shouted. Rivet zoomed away through the falling rubble. He dived through the arch, back into the main temple complex, rocketing past crumbling pillars and keeping close to Spike's tail.

Suddenly, Max heard a cry cut through the echoing crash of falling rock. "Stop! Help!" It came from somewhere to their right.

Rivet turned at the sound, tugging Max down a flight of steps to find a broad figure in a silver cloak, hunched low to the ground. The figure lifted its head and Max recognised General Phero. Thick chains bound the Gustadian's arms and legs to bolts driven into the floor.

"Max!" Phero cried. "The temple is collapsing. We must get out!" Max scanned the Gustadian's features, looking for any sign of a trick.

"How do we know it's really him?" Lia asked, as she arrived on Spike.

"We'll just have to hope it is," Max said. "We can't risk leaving the real Phero here! Rivet – can you break those chains?"

"Yes, Max!" Rivet barked. Max let go of his dogbot, and Rivet quickly chomped through the general's bonds.

The general rose and pointed towards a crack in the far wall. "That way! Quick!" he cried, his voice almost drowned out by a

tremendous boom from above. Max glanced up to see a huge section of the vaulted ceiling break away and crash towards him.

"Grab onto my dogbot!" he told the general. Max gripped Rivet's back alongside the big Gustadian. Rivet's motors whirred and he shot away, tugging Max and General

Phero through a pummelling hail of rock. Spike and Lia shot ahead. Max could hardly breathe in the choking silt, and soon he could see nothing but grey stone falling all around them. He glanced up. Terror gripped his heart and squeezed. A giant slab of rock was crashing towards him, so close he could make out the lines of its carving. *We're going to be crushed!*

CHAPTER EIGHT

A NEW NEMESIS

Max clung to his speeding dogbot, shoulder to shoulder with General Phero, silty water whooshing past his gills, and the sound of rumbling filling his ears. He held his breath, expecting any second to feel a deadly blow from the crushing weight of rock tumbling towards him. Ahead, he could just make out the silvery form of Spike, streaking through the crack in the temple wall. He gritted his teeth. *Please let us get out!*

Rivet dived through the crack behind

Spike, yanking Max and General Phero out into open water and the darkness of Shadowreach. A terrifying roar echoed behind them.

"Did it, Max!" Rivet barked, coming to rest on a rocky ledge.

Max let go of his dogbot, his hands shaking with relief as he dismounted alongside General Phero. "Good boy, Riv!" he said, patting Rivet's back. Lia and Spike swam to Max's side, and General Phero turned to face them.

"Thank you, both of you," the general said. His translated words echoed from a silver medallion around his neck. "I had almost given up hope of escaping. How did you find me?"

"We followed a man called Kade," Max said. "He impersonated you and planted a bomb at the Sumaran peace conference.

Luckily no one was hurt, but the conference is in chaos. Kade made it look like you ran away, so everyone blames you."

Phero nodded gravely. "Perhaps I *am* partly to blame. I knew Kade was hungry for power, but I never believed he would stoop to this." The general slumped onto a large boulder. His pale face looked tired and worn.

Max took a seat at Phero's side with Rivet,

and Lia floated before them on Spike.

The general sighed. "Kade once led an uprising against me. I showed mercy when his bid for power failed, and sent him into exile. If I had known what he was capable of, he would be rotting in a dungeon now."

"Kade has some of the most advanced tech I've ever seen," Max said. "Where did it come from?"

"He made it himself," Phero said. "He was once my head scientist. He perfected our glue guns, and made impressive headway with teleportation technology. But he went too far. Even burning his face in an accident didn't quell his ambition. He wanted us to use his technology to take over the Delta Quadrant, but I saw little profit in such a war. I sent Kade and his men packing. They must have used their shape-shifting technology to infiltrate Sumara and learn of the legend of Deepholm. They ambushed my sub on its way to the peace conference, and brought me here." The general's face twisted into a scowl. "Kade took pleasure in telling me his plans before leaving me to die. He intends to use the four Robobeasts he has created from the temple guardians to sow chaos, divide the Delta Alliance and forge a Gustadian empire."

"Well, he's already made pretty good headway," Max said. "You're going to have some serious explaining to do back in Sumara if we're going to avoid a war."

Phero shook his head. "I don't think any amount of explanation will do at this stage. No, Kade himself must confess. That is the only way there will be peace."

"Well, he won't confess without a fight," Max said, patting the butt of his blaster.

"He won't give up my mother's ring, either," Lia said. "And we need that more than ever to control the temple guardians. But we can't leave that giant worm on the loose! We'll have to deactivate Gort before we go after Kade."

"What do you mean?" Max asked. "Gort's buried under a mountain of rock. I think it's well and truly deactivated."

Lia shook her head. "Listen," she said, pointing towards the rock face. Max heard a low grating rumble coming from deep within the cliff – the sound of metal blades, boring through rock. His skin prickled with fear. The sound seemed to be moving upwards, towards the seabed above the chasm.

"I cannot stay here any longer," General Phero said. "Kade means to overthrow my government and begin a war. He has already sent men back to Gustados. But there is a vehicle bay with a number of craft hidden in a cave below us. I must go at once if I am to prevent another attack on Sumara."

"Then go!" Lia said. "And quickly!"

The general nodded. Then he smiled. "I seem to remember you two have a remarkable talent for overcoming robotic snakes. Let us hope you are as successful with this worm."

Max grinned and nodded. "Leave Gort to us. We have a perfect track record of defeating Robobeasts, and we're not about to let that change." He listened again to the hideous churning sound from deep within the rock. *I hope not, anyway…*

General Phero waved them farewell and disappeared into the cave below. Meanwhile, Max retrieved the aquasphere from where they had left it. He and Rivet clambered inside, and they headed up the chasm wall, with Spike and Lia at their side. When they reached an overhang just below the lip, they stopped. The sound of crunching rock had fallen silent.

"Gort must be up there somewhere," Lia said, frowning up at the chasm edge.

"Are you ready?" Max asked, his hand on the aquasphere blaster controls.

Lia nodded. "Ready."

Together, they crested the rocky ledge. Max found himself looking out over a wide, sandy plain covered with rippling dunes the colour of ash, which were bathed in shimmering light. Max could see the occasional outcrop of stone rising above the seabed, and a few brittle-looking coral trees. But there was no sign of Gort.

Suddenly, a hideous slithering sound from below made the hairs on Max's arms prickle. He tightened his grip on the controls.

"He must have been waiting for us underground!" Lia cried. "He's coming!"

Max tugged at his steering, angling the

aquasphere steeply upwards. Lia and Spike shot away from the seabed, just as a great plume of sand exploded below. Max glanced down to see the monstrous worm burst from the sand, its vast body snaking upwards, toothed pincers sticking straight out on either side of its round, gaping mouth, revealing the churning blenders inside.

CHAPTER NINE

PARALYSED

Max slammed the aquasphere forwards, terror knifing through his guts. In his rear viewer, he saw Spike speed away from the monster's crushing jaws just as they snapped shut, narrowly missing the swordfish's tail.

The vast worm let out an angry hiss, then sucked itself back into its hole, leaving nothing but a faint dip in the sand to show where it had appeared.

Lia and Spike swooped to Max's side. "It can sense our vibrations," she said.

Max nodded. "We have to keep away from the seabed."

They looked down, scanning the grey wasteland.

A loud whoosh from behind them sent an electric shock of fear through Max. He hit the sphere's thruster, his stomach flipping at the sudden rush of speed, then glanced in the rear viewer. Gort's muscular body shot out from the sand. Its long pincers snatched towards them, and Max could hear the whir of the deadly blades in its throat. He could see the current they made pulling at Lia's hair as she and Spike sped from the Robobeast.

We're too fast for it! Max thought with a swell of triumph. But then he saw the blue stone in Gort's throat glow bright. The vast worm dipped its head, and the two pincers on either side flicked. Several of the sharp teeth that lined the pincers flew free, slicing through the water like darts.

"Lia! Look out!" Max cried. But it was too late. Max's heart lurched as a tooth bit deep into the pale skin of Lia's shoulder. Another sliced into Spike's side.

"Lia and Spike hurt!" Rivet barked. More teeth pattered against the aquasphere's plexiglass sides, falling harmlessly to the seabed.

Lia put a hand to the dart with a puzzled frown. Then her eyes flickered shut and she slumped across Spike's back.

"NO!" Max roared. At the same moment, Spike's body went rigid and his eyes glazed over. The swordfish looked like a fisherman's cold, dead catch. Gort cannoned towards him, mouth open wide to swallow the Merryn princess and her pet whole.

Rage and horror boiled inside Max. He spun the aquasphere around, setting his weapons to rapid fire, and slammed blast

after blast into the giant worm's body.

Gort jolted to a stop. Its vast head lashed from side to side and it screeched with pain. Max kept firing, peppering the howling worm while Lia and Spike drifted lifelessly through the water. Finally, when Max thought his blasters were about to fail, Gort burrowed headfirst into the sand. Max glanced at the shallow crater left by the worm and shuddered. Gort could reappear at any moment. But he'd have to take that chance. He flipped the lid of the aquasphere open and shot out towards Lia and Spike. "Come on, Riv! We have to help them!"

Lia's body lolled lifelessly over Spike's back as the swordfish sailed silently through the water, losing height fast.

Rivet dipped his nose under Spike's belly, and Max put out a hand to steady Lia. He felt a twinge of hope as he saw her gills flickering. *She's alive!*

Max scanned the seabed, looking for a rock large enough to keep Lia and Spike safe from Gort. "Over there, Riv!" he said, pointing to a table-shaped outcrop. Rivet nosed Spike on towards the rock, then let him drift gently down onto it. Lia's body felt cold and stiff as Max eased her from Spike's back and settled her beside her faithful pet. Her face was so pale that her closed eyelids looked like white shells, veined with blue. Gort's tooth still pierced her shoulder. Max tugged it free, leaving a small, bloodless hole. The tip of the tooth was blackened with toxin. Rivet yanked the dart from Spike's side with his teeth and spat it out.

"Poison, Max!" Rivet barked.

Max looked at his friends, lying still and silent on their bed of rock, and anger welled inside him so powerful it took his breath away. *They're still breathing,* he told himself. *I just have to protect them from Gort. I have to free the guardian from Kade's evil power. But how can I get that blue stone from its throat?*

Max glanced down at the black-tipped

tooth in his hand and, suddenly, he had an idea.

"Rivet, look after Lia and Spike," Max told his dogbot. "I'm going to give that worm a taste of its own medicine." He drew his hyperblade and dived towards the seabed, where two black-tipped teeth lay. Max swam towards them with gentle strokes so as not to stir the sand. He picked them up, tucking one into his belt, and holding the other carefully in his free hand. Then he stamped down hard on the seabed, sending up a swirling eddy of silt. Nothing happened.

"Come on, Gort!" Max shouted, stomping heavily again. "I'm still here! You didn't get me!" Suddenly, he felt the sand beneath him shift, and a faint slithering sound reached his ears. *Got you!* Max dived sideways and crouched, the black-tipped tooth in his fist drawn back, ready to strike.

The sand exploded outwards in a wave, pattering against Max's body as the vast muscular worm shot upwards. Acting on instinct, Max leapt forwards and drove the point in his hand hard into a chink between the worm's armoured segments, as it rushed past. The tooth was jerked from Max's hand, stuck fast in the creature's hide, as the monstrous worm climbed higher. It let out

a wild howl of rage, shuddering all over, its triangular legs quivering. Max looked up to see its blunt head angle back downwards towards him in a deadly U-turn, pincers wide, showing the whirring blades in its throat.

Max drew the other tooth from his belt and plunged it deep into the thick, shuddering hide before him, just before it whipped up out of reach. The monster's wide mouth plunged towards him, the deadly blades so close that Max could feel their current. Max waited a heartbeat longer, then kicked away, his arms and legs pumping in the water.

CRUNCH!

Gort's head struck the seabed just behind him, sending up a whirling vortex of sand. Max turned to see the Robobeast lift its head, spewing out a choking cloud of sand. It shook and writhed, hissing furiously. But

Max could see that its movements were slowing. The worm's thrashing calmed to a gentle sway, then its vast body went slack. It lurched sideways and toppled gradually down onto the seabed, throwing up clouds of sand. Finally, it lay almost still, its legs and feelers quivering, its pincers clamped together like clenched teeth. The whine of the blades in its throat faltered, and at last fell silent.

Max edged towards the worm, his hyperblade held out before him and his heart thundering against his ribs. His eyes were fixed on the blue gem at the Robobeast's throat.

Snick! He drove the sharp tip of his hyperblade down between the edge of the stone and the armour. The gem flew free and Max caught it.

Gort let out a long, contented hiss. Its body

sagged further into the sand. Its twitching feelers fell still, and the shiny plates of metal clamped to its body tumbled away onto the seabed.

It's asleep! I've beaten it. But Max couldn't feel any joy in his victory – not with Lia and Spike still sick from Gort's toxin. Max swam to the rock where he'd left Rivet to guard their bodies.

"Worm gone to sleep, Max!" Rivet barked happily.

"That's right, Riv," Max said. "But how are Spike and Lia?"

"Sleeping too, Max!" Rivet barked again. Max saw that his dogbot was right. Where Lia's body had been lying stiff and pale, her spear still grasped in her hand, now she looked peaceful. A rosy glow had spread to her cheeks. Spike's fins were flickering, and Max noticed he was floating just above the rock.

Max dropped to his knees at Lia's side, relief flooding through him. He gave her a gentle shake, grinning as her eyes flickered open.

She sat up slowly, frowning. "What happened?" she asked, then her eyes shot wide open with alarm. "Gort shot me!"

Max nodded. "It paralysed you. Thank goodness its toxins have worn off. How do you feel?"

"Fine!" Lia said. She glanced at Spike, and smiled. "He's dreaming." She scanned the sandy seascape around them, stopping when she saw Gort's sleeping form.

"Is it over?" she said. Max nodded, showing her the gem in his hand.

"Gort's no longer a problem," he said. "But Kade is still on the loose with the other three temple guardians under his control. And he won't rest until he has control of the Delta Quadrant."

Lia nodded, her expression suddenly grave. "So you and I are all that stands between our people and a deadly war," she said.

At her side, Rivet wagged his tail. "More Sea Quests!" Rivet barked.

Max smiled and patted his dogbot's head. "That's right, Riv. So let's get on our way!"

THE END

Don't miss Max's next Sea Quest adventure,
when he faces

HYDROR
THE OCEAN HUNTER

978 1 40834 097 4

IF YOU LIKE SEA QUEST, YOU'LL LOVE BEAST QUEST!

Series 1: COLLECT THEM ALL!

An evil wizard has enchanted the magical beasts of Avantia. Only a true hero can free the beasts and save the land. Is Tom the hero Avantia has been waiting for?

FERNO
THE FIRE DRAGON

978 1 84616 483 5

SEPRON
THE SEA SERPENT

978 1 84616 482 8

ARCTA
THE MOUNTAIN GIANT

978 1 84616 484 2

TAGUS
THE HORSE MAN

978 1 84616 486 6

NANOOK
THE SNOW MONSTER

978 1 84616 485 9

EPOS
THE FLAME BIRD

978 1 84616 487 3

DON'T MISS THE BRAND NEW SERIES OF:

Series 17: THE BROKEN STAR

978 1 40834 076 9

978 1 40834 080 6

978 1 40834 082 0

978 1 40834 084 4

COMING SOON